DRAGON
FINDS FRIENDS

BY LYN DOVE & ILLUSTRATED BY MELISSA WOLF

Once in the deep dark of the world

lived a sad, lonely dragon.

He didn't have a name because no one had

ever cared enough about him to give him one.

Not even his Mum!

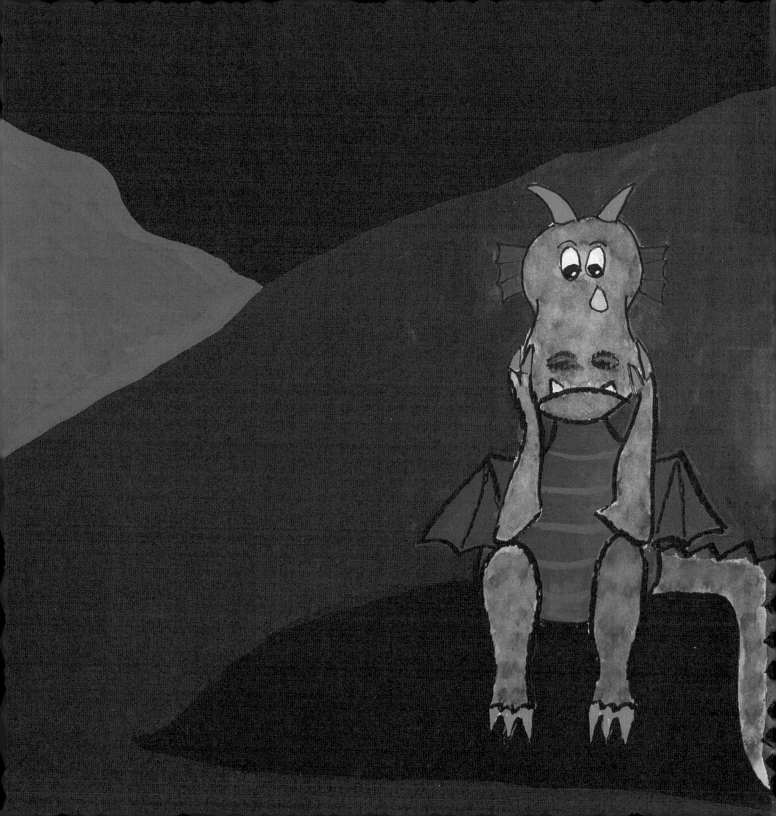

As he lay alone in the darkness, he started to wonder if somehow, somewhere there might be someone who could become his friend.

Someone to talk to,

someone to share with,

someone to care.

Feeling a bit scared, he set off on his adventure.

He felt better already because now he had a plan.

Slowly, he started to dig with his massive front

claws, aiming upwards from his black cave in the rock.

Somehow it seemed the right thing to do.

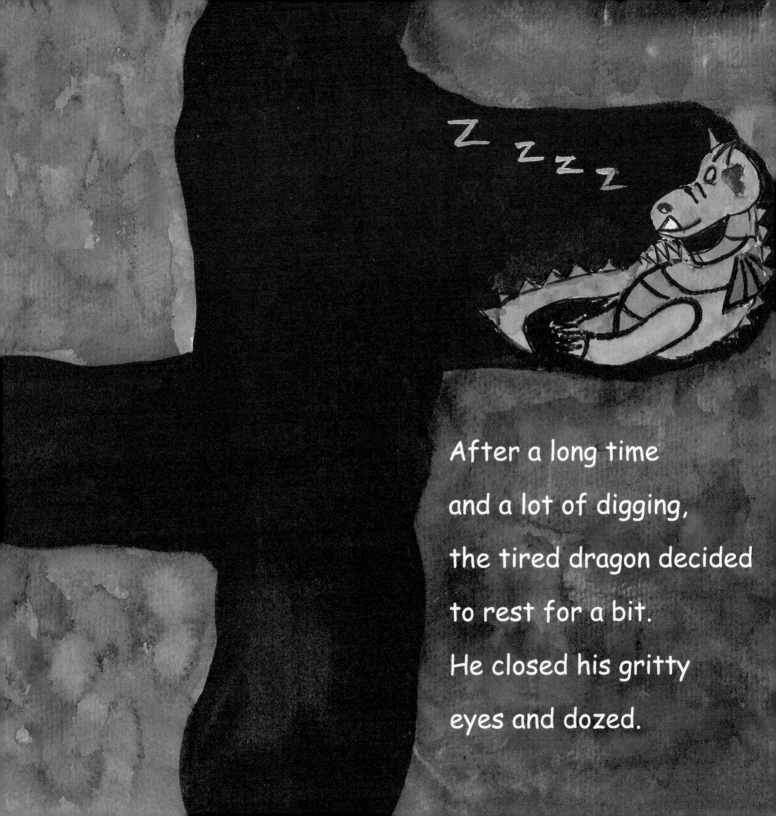

After a long time
and a lot of digging,
the tired dragon decided
to rest for a bit.
He closed his gritty
eyes and dozed.

Much later, he woke up with a start! Something was moving just above him.

He held his breath in the darkness, not sure whether to be afraid, excited or both! He strained his ears to listen because obviously he couldn't see a thing in the dark.

The something came closer and closer until...

...a squeaky but bossy voice said,

"I know you're there —

I can hear you breathing!"

The dragon was so surprised he let out a
HOT spurt of flame
from his HUGE nostrils.

And, in the light from the fire,

he saw a tiny mouse no bigger

than his smallest claw!

But before the dragon could do or say anything, the mouse climbed onto his head and sat just inside his left ear.

"I think it's safer here," squeaked the mouse.

"Your fire is very hot!"

"S s s sorry," the dragon stammered, finding

his voice at last.

"I didn't mean to do that — you scared me!"

Then the dragon found his courage and explained how sad and lonely he was living in the deep, dark of the world.

Taking a deep breath, careful not to breathe any fire, he said,

"Will you be my friend?"

Bravely, the mouse answered,

"Well... maybe we can help each other.

My little legs are very tired after all this digging.

I've been trying to make a hole big enough for

my family and it's taking a

VERY

LONG

TIME."

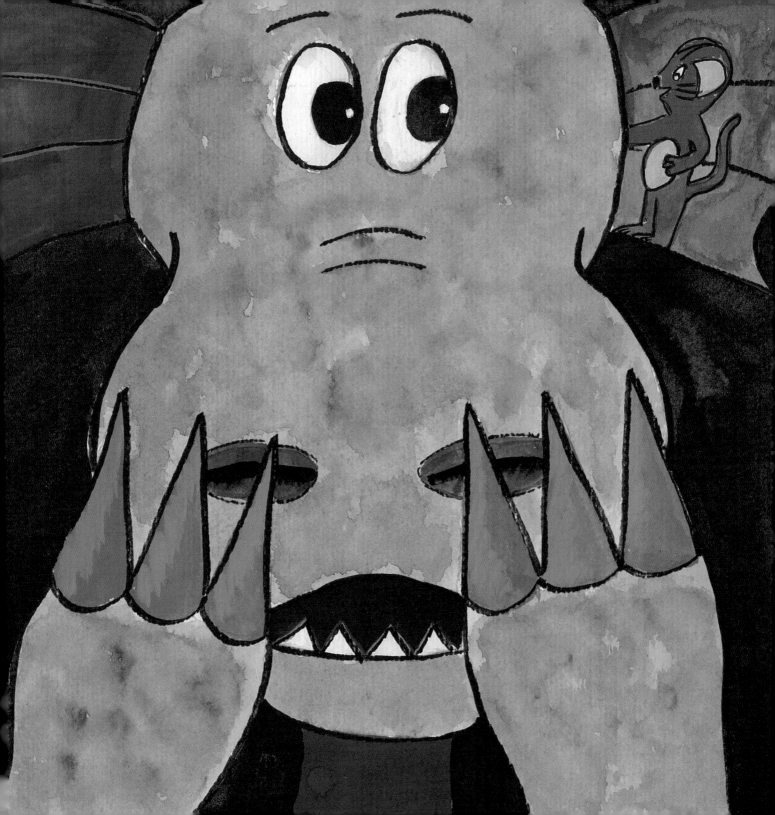

"I'll help," replied the dragon eagerly.

"My claws are very strong

and I could make you a hole

any size you like."

So the tiny mouse nestled into the dragon's warm left ear and gave instructions for the digging, while the dragon listened carefully to make sure he did everything right. He liked the squeaky sound of the mousy voice and the tickle of soft fur in his leathery ear.

Finally, the hole was shaped to the mouse's satisfaction.

"Right!" said the mouse.

"I'll go and get my family and show them their new home.

Thank you very much for all your digging...

Er...

What did you say your name was?"

And the dragon explained how and why he didn't have a name.

"Well we can't have that," responded the mouse bossily.

"I shall call you Digger because you dug this splendid hole.

It will suit you very well as you have such magnificent claws."

So the mouse scurried away and Digger,

who was very proud of his new name,

waited patiently in the dark, silent hole,

hoping that Tiny would return soon.

He dug and scraped
another much bigger,
more spacious hole
with a high ceiling
and smooth walls.

He was just finishing the job

when he heard a scratching sound

and the babble of cheerful voices.

Tiny appeared

with what seemed like

hundreds of mice

all chattering together.

Digger's heart missed a beat...

Oh no! Tiny didn't seem to like the big hole

he'd just dug next door to the mouse hole.

"I was just going to say," said Tiny,

"that maybe the mouse hole needs to be a bit

bigger as there are so many of us.

And now I see you have already dug a

LARGE hole right next door.

What a clever dragon you are!"

Tiny liked the second hole.

"Now there will be room for everyone,"

squeaked Tiny excitedly.

So the mice and the dragon moved in as neighbours.

Tiny's big family grew even bigger because Digger

was always there to protect them from harm.

But better still,

Digger was never sad or lonely again because he had so many

new little friends, who just loved to take it in turns

to sit in his ear and tell him stories of times gone by.

First Published in the UK in 2022
ISBN 9798357997258

Text copyright © Lyn Dove 2022
Illustration copyright © Melissa Wolf 2022

Printed in Great Britain
by Amazon

18643121R00022